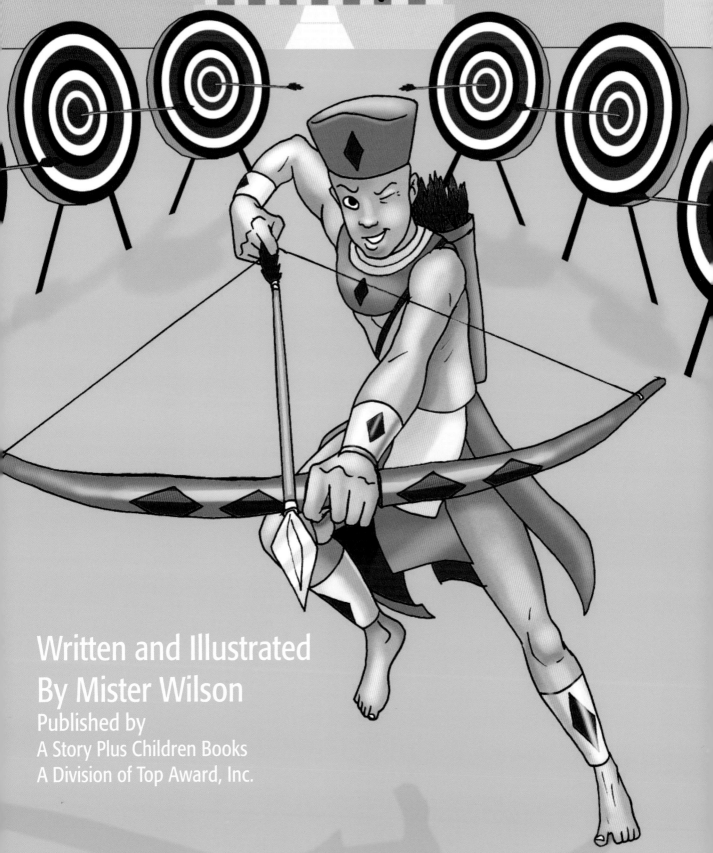

Arron The Royal Archer

Written and Illustrated
By Mister Wilson

Published by
A Story Plus Children Books
A Division of Top Award, Inc.

Coordination and convergence by Rhonda V. Maddox.

Plus Activity development by George H. Wilson II.

 Color and Detail by Christopher J Neal, Kai Studios.

Visit our website at www.astoryplus.com for information about our books.

ISBN-0-97784773X

Library of Congress Control Number: 2007905585

Wilson, Mister

Arron the Royal Archer/ Mister Wilson

Printed in Malaysia

Arron The Royal Archer

Dedicated

To My Sister

Mrs. Barbara Wilson-Turner

Who always reminds me that I am loved.

And always to
My Wife, Vanessa and my children: Kwandra, Cleshea,
Asia, Alaina,
and
George II.

Thanks

Long ago, in the land of the birth of the bow and arrow, there was a young boy named Arron. Arron was poor and lived deep in the forest of a great kingdom. Food was hard to find, so Arron and his family went to sleep many nights without a meal. But whenever Arron could find food he would always share some with an old storyteller.

"Storyteller, here is some bread," offered Arron
"Thank you Arron," said the Storyteller.
"Is the story of the archers true?" asked Arron.
"Oh yes! Every year there is a contest and men travel to the castle to compete to become one of the King's Royal Archers. The ten best shooters and their families get to live within the palace walls and eat from the King's table," answered the story teller.
"I will build a bow and one day I will be good enough to enter the contest!" stated Arron.

2

Arron began to build his bow and arrow using small branches, a strand of rope and some feathers. And after many failed tries, he finally succeeded in building a very good bow and arrows.

3

Arron made a target of straw and tied it to a tree. He practiced from sun up till sunset everyday.

After a time he was able to hit the center of the target with every arrow he shot.

Becoming a good shot made it easier for Arron to find food. He began to have successful hunts each day with the bow and arrow. Arron could now provide food for his family most nights before they lay down to sleep.

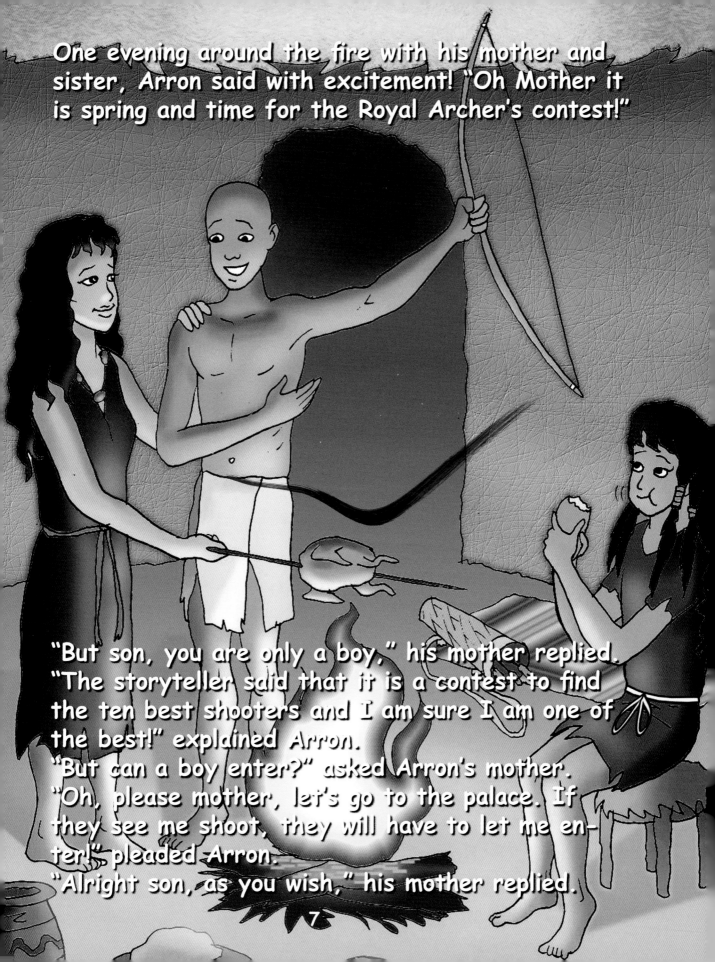

One evening around the fire with his mother and sister, Arron said with excitement! "Oh Mother it is spring and time for the Royal Archer's contest!"

"But son, you are only a boy," his mother replied. "The storyteller said that it is a contest to find the ten best shooters and I am sure I am one of the best!" explained Arron.
"But can a boy enter?" asked Arron's mother.
"Oh, please mother, let's go to the palace. If they see me shoot, they will have to let me en-ter!" pleaded Arron.
"Alright son, as you wish," his mother replied.

Arron, his mother and little sister packed what little they owned into sacks. They would have to rely on hunting and gathering for food on their journey.

They were all excited to be going to the palace
for the Royal Archer's contest. So the next morning before the sun was high in the sky they eagerly
started on their journey.

After many days and nights of walking, they came upon a great palace. They could not believe their eyes, the palace was so beautiful. Many people had come from far away for the royal archer contest.

"It is as the storyteller said, that many would come to the palace to compete in the Royal Archer contest," said Arron.
"It does appear so," replied his mother.
"And the storyteller said that if I should win, we may live within these palace walls and eat from the King's table," said Arron.

Hundreds of people camped outside the palace walls. Arron and his family found a small space to build a fire to wait for the morning of the contest.

12

Before the sun had come up, Arron had awakened. He made sure he was first in line. But when the other men arrived they began pushing him to the back of the line. "Move back, boy this is not child's play!" "Get out of the line boy! This contest is for men!" the men shouted angrily.

None of the men would allow Arron to stand in front of them. So, Arron was pushed all the way to the end of the line.

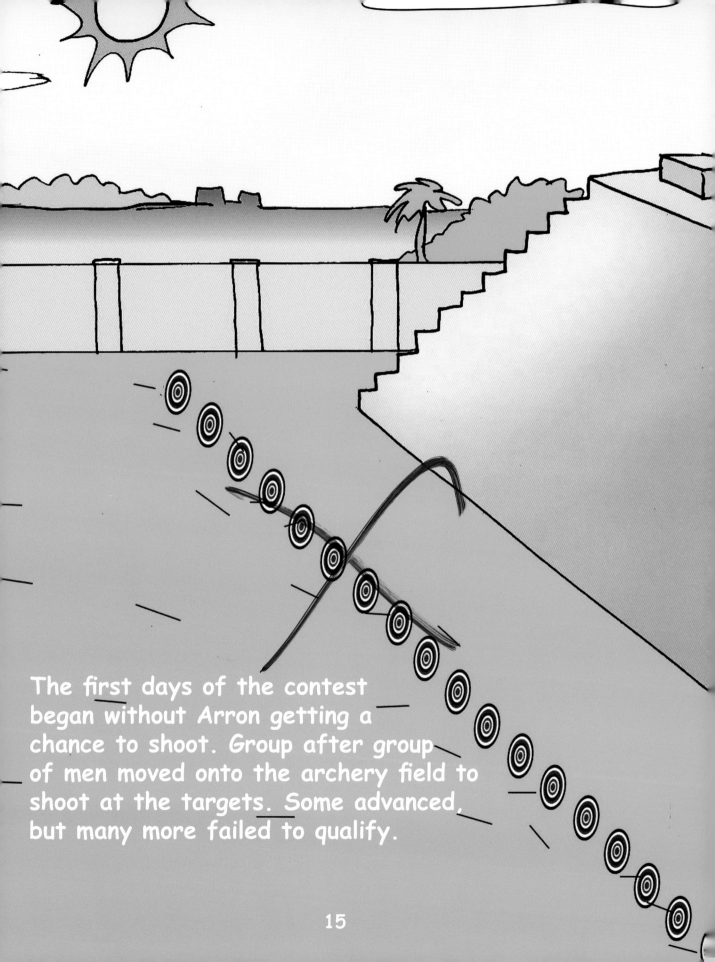

The first days of the contest began without Arron getting a chance to shoot. Group after group of men moved onto the archery field to shoot at the targets. Some advanced, but many more failed to qualify.

The final group of men were preparing to shoot at the targets. The King, as always, came to see the best of the archers shoot. He was carried in on a throne lead by his guards.

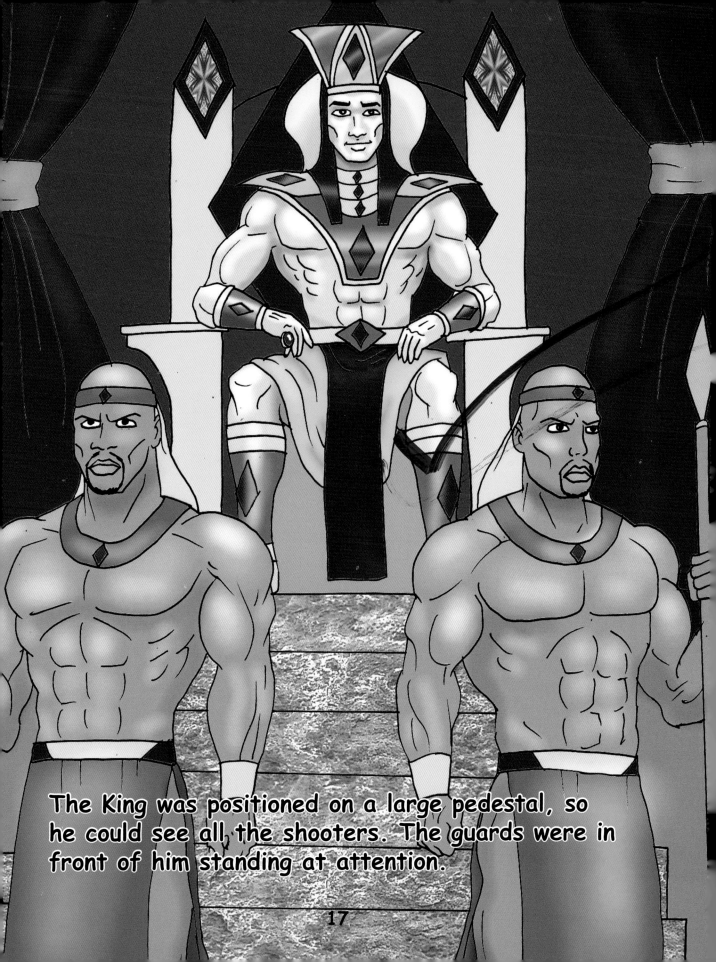

The King was positioned on a large pedestal, so he could see all the shooters. The guards were in front of him standing at attention.

As the final groups lined up to shoot, Arron tried once again to hold his place in line. But the men only became angry with him. "Are you the same boy that we spoke to before?" someone asked.

"This competition is for men who have families to care for," the men shouted.
"I have to take care of my mother and sister," Arron replied.
"Give me that bow and arrows!" yelled the men. The men snatched the bow and arrows from Arron and threw him to the ground. They took Arron's bow and arrows and broke them into pieces!

"Now go and play boy!"
the men said angrily.

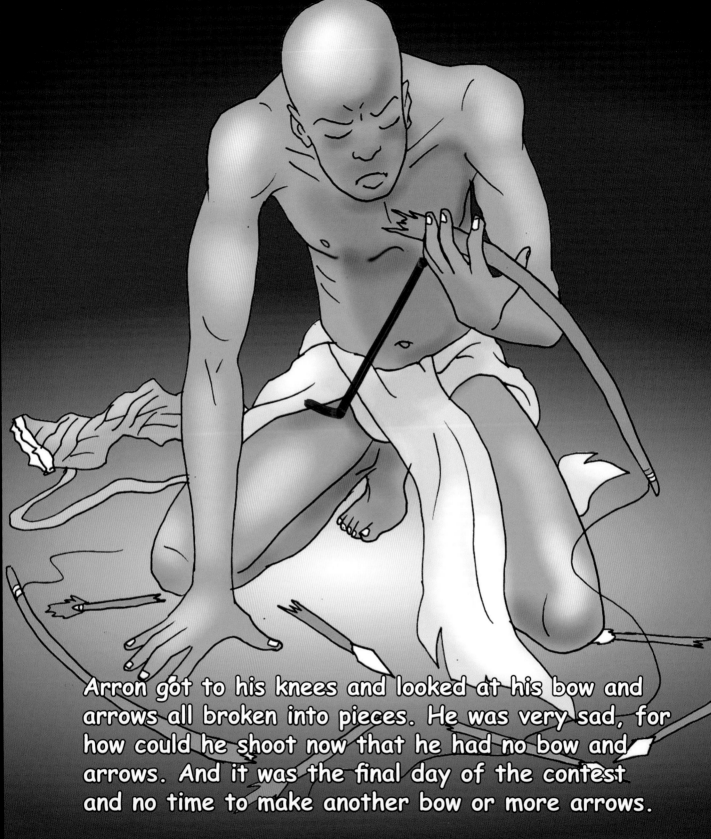

Arron got to his knees and looked at his bow and arrows all broken into pieces. He was very sad, for how could he shoot now that he had no bow and arrows. And it was the final day of the contest and no time to make another bow or more arrows.

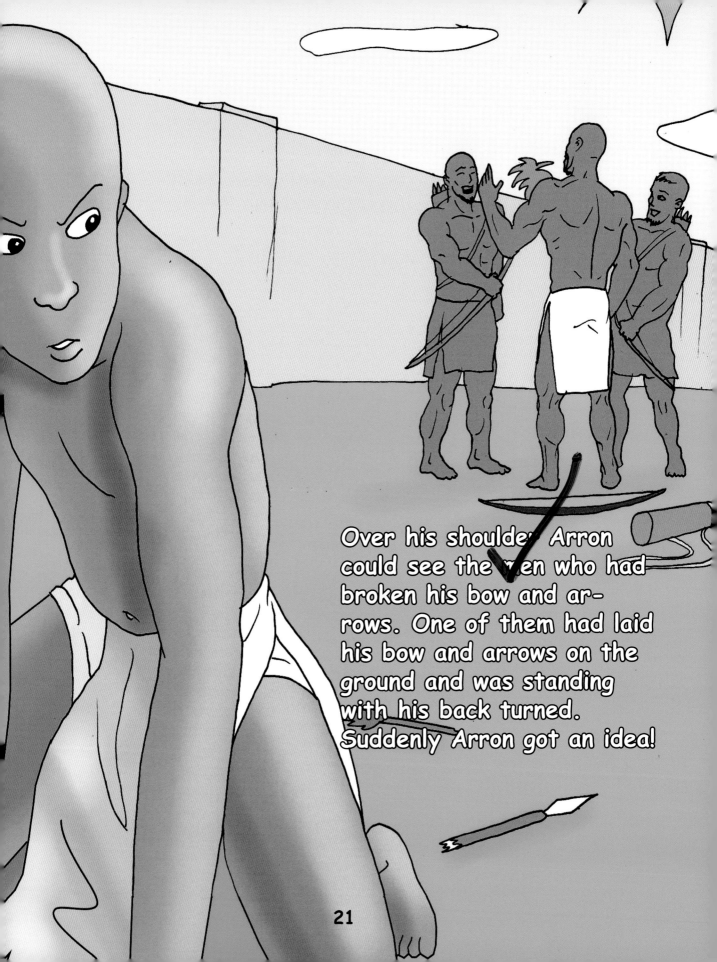

Over his shoulder Arron could see the men who had broken his bow and arrows. One of them had laid his bow and arrows on the ground and was standing with his back turned. Suddenly Arron got an idea!

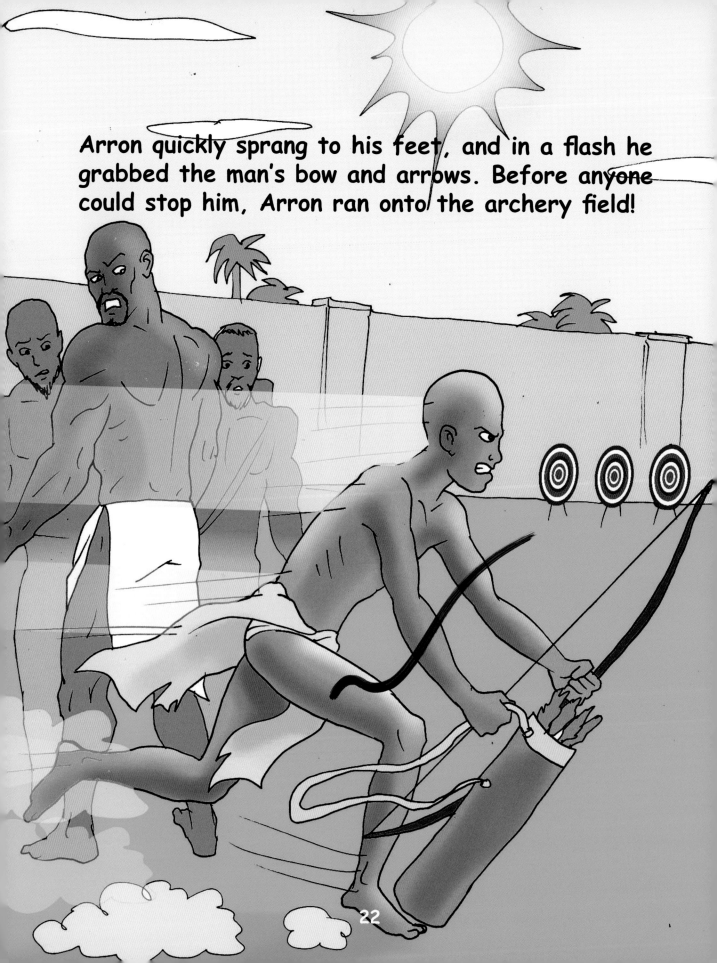

Arron quickly sprang to his feet, and in a flash he grabbed the man's bow and arrows. Before anyone could stop him, Arron ran onto the archery field!

The men and the King's guards chased after Arron. Arron knew that this was his only chance to prove that he should be allowed to enter the contest. So he quickly loaded and shot five arrows toward five targets.

The arrows arrived and struck each of the five targets in the center of the bull's eye almost perfectly.

The guards captured Arron and brought him to kneel before the pedestal of the King. The King stood up in amazement and commanded. "Go and bring me those five targets!"

"Right away my King," replied the servant and he turned to retrieve the targets.

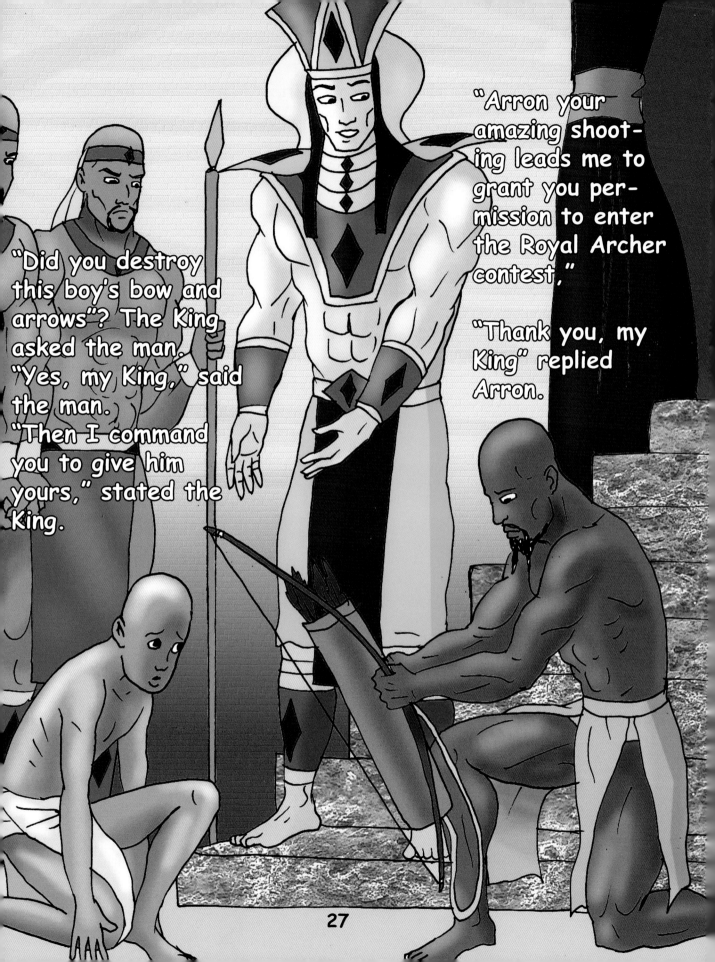

"Did you destroy this boy's bow and arrows"? The King asked the man.
"Yes, my King," said the man.
"Then I command you to give him yours," stated the King.

"Arron your amazing shooting leads me to grant you permission to enter the Royal Archer contest,"

"Thank you, my King" replied Arron.

27

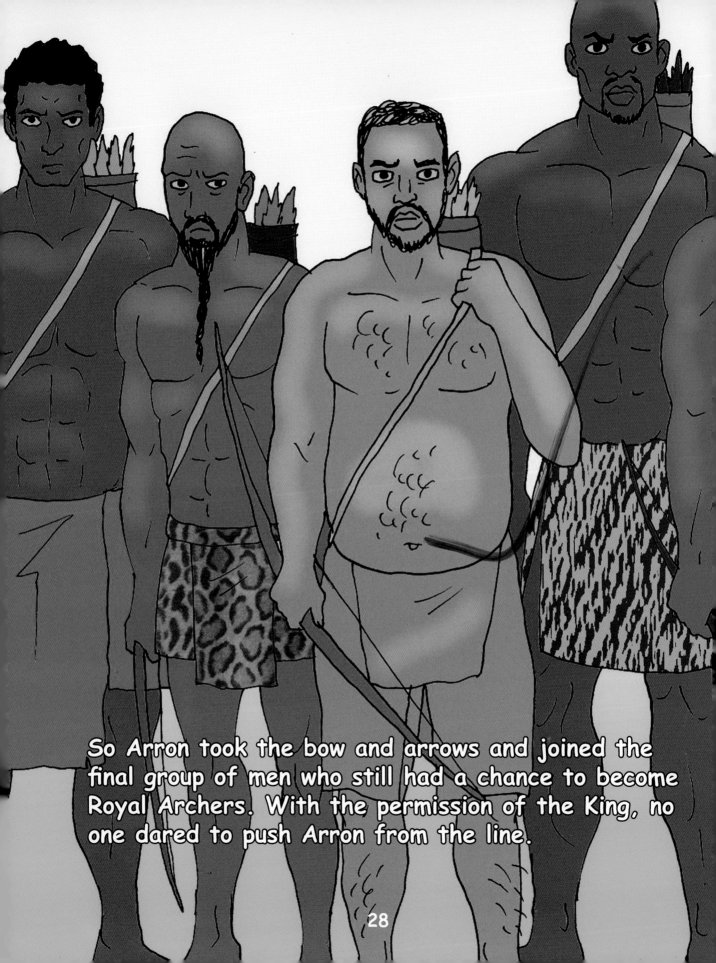

So Arron took the bow and arrows and joined the final group of men who still had a chance to become Royal Archers. With the permission of the King, no one dared to push Arron from the line.

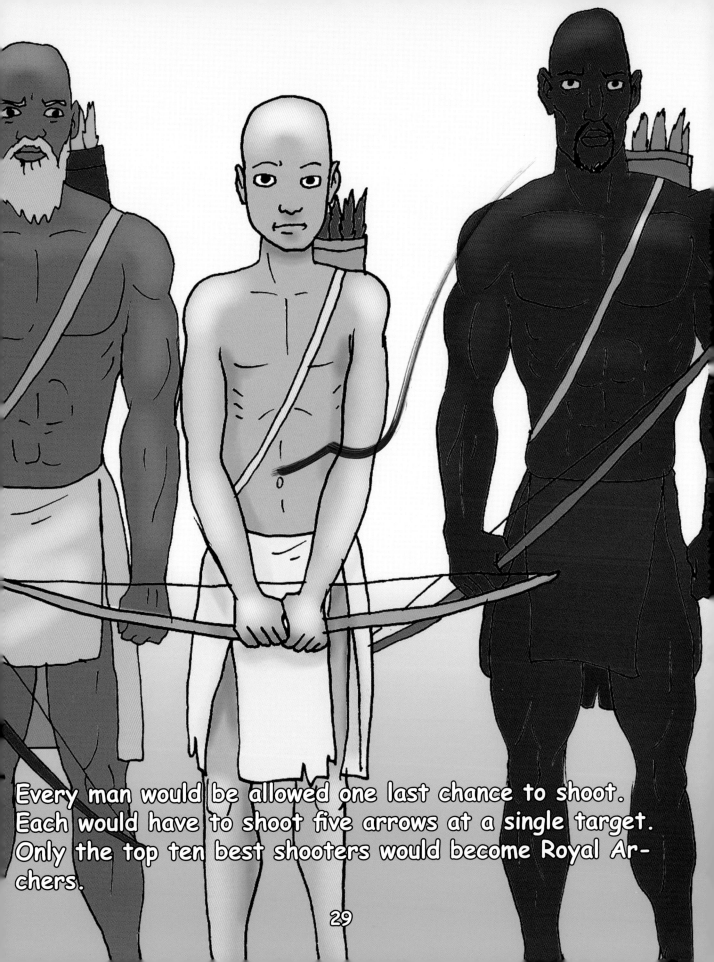

Every man would be allowed one last chance to shoot. Each would have to shoot five arrows at a single target. Only the top ten best shooters would become Royal Archers.

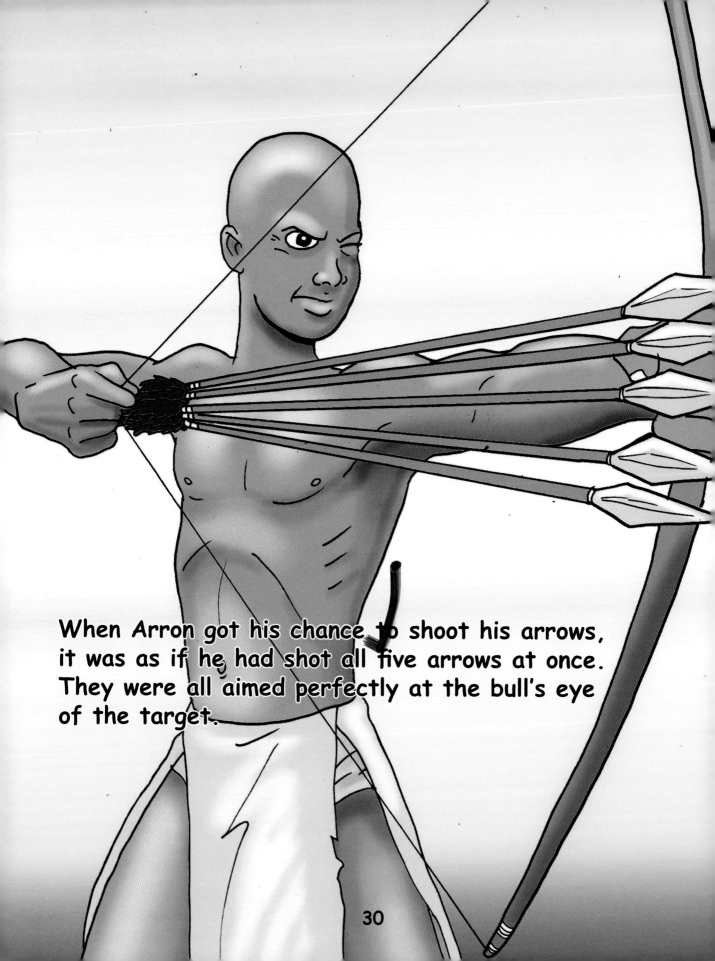

When Arron got his chance to shoot his arrows, it was as if he had shot all five arrows at once. They were all aimed perfectly at the bull's eye of the target.

Each of Arron's five arrows took a straight and true path to the target. They landed perfectly in the center of the bull's eye. Arron was the best shooter in the competition!

The ten best shooters were given the uniform of the King's Royal Archer. The Royal Archers were also given new silk clothing for the members of their families to wear.

All the new Royal Archers left the palace walls excited. They hurried to share their good news with their families. "I did it! I did it!" Arron shouted as he ran towards his family.

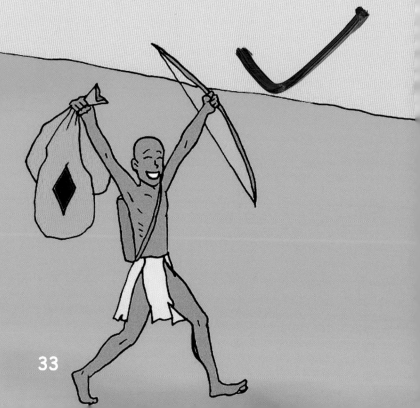

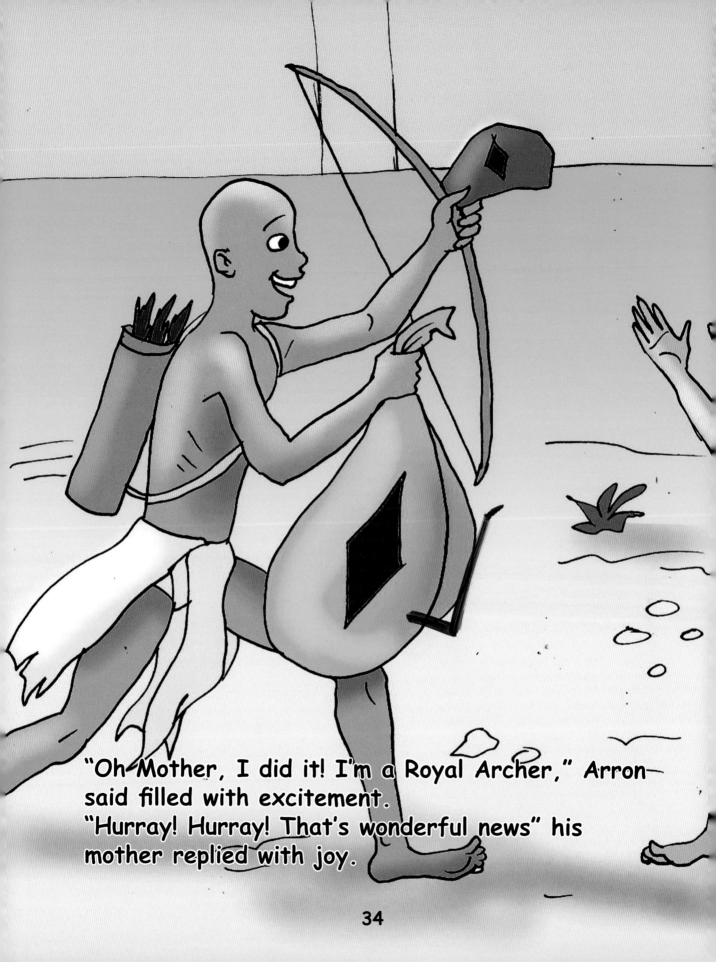

"Oh Mother, I did it! I'm a Royal Archer," Arron said filled with excitement.
"Hurray! Hurray! That's wonderful news" his mother replied with joy.

"So will we move inside the palace walls and eat from the King's table?" his sister asked.
"Oh yes sister and here are our new clothes to wear to the palace," Arron replied proudly.

35

The huge table was filled with plenty of things to eat and their wonderful smells filled the air. "Oh Mother, I have never seen or smelled the food of a King before, it looks too good to eat!" said Arron's sister.

36

"You can thank your brother for he fought hard to get into the contest. He refused to be denied a chance to provide for you and your mother. Now you shall live inside the palace walls and eat the finest foods in the Kingdom," stated the King.

After the feast the King presented the new Royal Archers to the people of the Kingdom.

"And last, but not least, I present to you the best shooter in the contest. Arron the Royal Archer! And I declare by the words of this letter, that from this day forward, a Royal Archer will no longer be determined by age alone, but by the trueness of his arrows!" proclaimed the King.

All the people were filled with joy for the boy archer and chanted. "Arron the Royal Archer!"

Arron proved to be the best archer in the Kingdom and was the youngest to ever become a Royal Archer!

ARRON
THE
ROYAL ARCHER

PLUS!

PLUS!
CONTENT

PLUS!

MORALS OF EXCELLENCE

ARRON THE ROYAL ARCHER

"NO MATTER WHAT OBSTACLES YOU FACE, YOU CAN FIND A WAY TO OVERCOME THEM"

WHAT DID YOU LEARN FROM THE STORY?

WHAT DO WANT TO BECOME? AND WHAT WILL YOU HAVE TO OVERCOME?

BIO-GEO

Bow and Arrow uses

Hunting for Food
Sports
       *Target Shooting
       *Shooting for Distance
       *Game hunting
Weapon of War

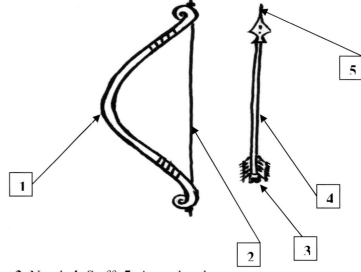

Parts Bow: 1. Curved wood **2.** Cord **Arrow: 3.** Notch **4.** Staff **5.** Arrowhead
Related: Atlatl, Sling, Whip bow, Spear, Javelin

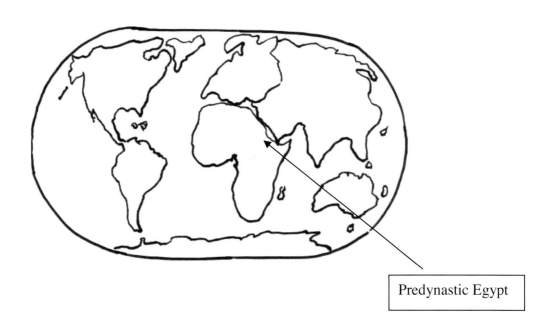

Predynastic Egypt

Place of Origin: Probably invented in predynastic Egypt.
Time of Origin: Late Paleolithic or early Mesolithic period

PLUS!

LEVEL 1 TEST
ARRON THE ROYAL ARCHER

MATCHING

1.  B is for_____

2.  C is for_____

3.  D is for_____

4.  A is for_____

5.  F is for_____

6.  T is for_____

COUNTING

7.  How many deer do you count?____

8.  How many bow & arrows do you count?_____

9.  How many targets do you count?_____

10. 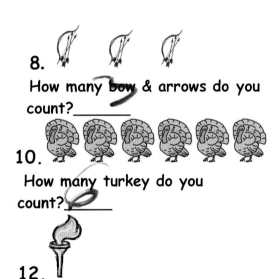 How many turkey do you count?_____

11.  How many castles do you count?_____2

12. How many flames do you count?_____

FINISHED_____7

ASP-5

PLUS!
COLORING PAGE
Please make a copy and color.

ASP-6

LEVEL 2 TEST
ARRON THE ROYAL ARCHER

Match the sentence with the correct word.

1. Who invited Arron to eat with him? _____   A. Spring

2. What did Arron use for a bow & arrow? ___   B. 5

3. How many men entered the competition? _____   C. 3

4. In what season did the competition take place?_____   D. Branches & Rope

5. How many targets did Arron shoot on the run? _____   E. hundreds

6. How many were in Arron's family? ___   F. King

TRUE & FALSE

7. Only twenty men entered the competition? _____

8. The royal archer competition was held in the bitter cold? _____

9. The royal archers were the safe guards of the city? _____

10. The King never attended the archer competition? _____

11. Arron shot five bulls eyes in all the targets while on the run? _____

12. Arron won a spot as a royal archer? _____

FINISHED____

WORD PUZZLE
Arron The Royal Archer

```
A H C J O D L D A T F X T H J
M R T S K U R X I I P H A F D
T A R G E T H I R E A R B F E
X P O O W V W E B Y L F L S X
J M F N W J M Q O C Z C E H I
Q H P C V M T N X K Y J M P W
L Y N I M V E T G P R C Y S G
B N V J M J V K I N M K W P F
R G D M Q O G Y D X C R I H W
E Y G O Z B D S C E A E I O T
E J B U B U D G L Z J H B J D
D E M B F P L T N C V T U X P
Q P B N W B S K T I A A R X L
G N I K L A Y Q V S K E D J Y
S I M V C J O I Y K N F M U L
```

ARROW   BIRD   BOW
CASTLE   DEER   FEATHER
FIRE   KING   KINGDOM
TARGET

PLUS!

Fun Facts
ARRON THE ROYAL ARCHER

1. The bow came into existence in prehistoric times.

2. The bow and arrow may have been invented by the ancient Egyptians.

3. "Self Bows" were present before the dynasties of Egypt

4. Some "Composite Bows" were evident in Egyptian ancient tombs.

5. Egyptian warriors shot bows and arrow from chariots.

6. The oldest bows known were discovered in Denmark in 1940.

7. Archers on horseback made the most dominant army.

8 English Kings made laws that all male must learn to use the longbow.

9. Each culture made its own type of bows.

10. A person who makes bows is called a bowyer.

11. The bow's elasticity gives it the power to project arrows.

12. Bow and arrow tournaments have been held since the middle ages.

13. The ancient uses of the bow were hunting for food and a weapon of   war.

14. The bow and arrow enabled people to kill animals from far away distances.

15. Today the bow and arrow are used for sport and hobbies.

16. A quiver is a pouch used to carry arrows.

17. Archery is the practice of using the bow and arrow.

18. Archery is currently and event in the Summer Olympic games.

19. Flight archery is shooting for distance not accuracy.

20. Field archery is shooting targets at varying distances in an open field.

21. The most common type of archery contest is target archery...

22. The targets are called buttresses and have color values and rings.

23. The bull's eye is located at the center of the buttress target.

24. An arrow that sticks in the bull's eye scores a perfect score of 10 points.

25. A person who practices the use of the bow and arrow is called an archer or bowman.

LEVEL 3 TEST
ARRON THE ROYAL ARCHER

1. Who invented the bow and arrow?

    A. Americans   B. Ancient Egyptians   C. Native Americans

2. The perfect bulls-eye score is represented by how many points?

    A. 25   B. 100   C. 10

3. Which one is <u>not</u> a part of the arrow?

    A. quiver   B. shaft   C. nock

4. Flight archery is for?

    A. distance   B. accuracy   C. speed

5. The bow and arrow is used to kill animals from?

    A. close up distances   B. from far away distances C. from in a cave

6. A quiver is?

    A. a pouch to hold arrows B. another name for a target C. part of
    the arrow

7. Archery is an event at the_____?

    A. Winter Olympics   B. Wimbledon   C. Summer Olympics

8. Field archery is for?

    A. targets at close range   B. targets at various distances C.
    targets far away

9. The most common type of archery contest is?

    A. flight archery   B. field archery   C. target archery

10. The bull's eye is located at the?

    A. center of the target   B. top of the target C. bottom of the
    target
FINISHED_____

PLUS!

SPELL & DEFINE

<u>ARRON THE ROYAL ARCHER</u>

Directions: Choose from the list below and learn to spell, define and use each word in a sentence. When using your resources (dictionary, encyclopedia, library, computer) it maybe helpful to use as your keywords <u>bow, arrow, target and archery.</u>

List #1	List # 2	List # 3	List # 4
1. Bow	1. Archery	1. Spear	1. Qualify
2. Arrow	2. Shaft	2. Shield	2. Score
3. String	3. Arrowhead	3. Guard	3. Skills
4. Stick	4. Bend	4. Solider	4. Expert
5. Hunt	5. Aim	5. Warrior	5. Craft
6. Kill	6. Attack	6. Marksman	6. Practice
7. Target	7. Circles	7. Sharpeshooter	7. Determination
8. Shoot	8. Direct Hit	8. Competition	8. Victory
9. Game	9. Mark	9. Winner	9. Defeat
10. Bullseye	10. Flight	10. Champion	10. Conquest

PLUS!

INSPIRATION

<u>ARRON THE ROYAL ARCHER</u>

<u>***ATTENTION:***</u> *THE ENTIRE LIST OF ITEMS REQUIRES PARENTAL APPROVAL AND SUPERVISION.*

<u>THINGS TO TRY</u>

1. <u>REAL LIFE</u>: VISIT A SPORTING GOODS STORE TO SEE A MODERN BOW AND ARROW SET.

2. <u>LIBRARY/BOOK STORE</u>: CHECK OUT OR BUY ANOTHER BOOK OR MAGAZINE TO READ ON BOW AND ARROW.

3. <u>COMPUTER</u>: LOCATE ONLINE SITES TO LEARN MORE ABOUT BOW AND ARROW.

4. <u>TELEVISION/RADIO</u>: PREVIEW SCHEDULED PROGRAMING TO IDENTIFY RELATED SUBJECT MATTERS.

5. <u>PRACTICAL</u>: TAKE AN ARCHERY CLASS OR TRY TO BUILD A BOW AND ARROWS FROM STICKS.

PLUS!
TEST ANSWERS
ARRON THE ROYAL ARCHER

LEVEL 1	LEVEL 2	LEVEL 3
1. BOW & ARROW	1. F	1. B
2. CASTLE	2. D	2. C
3. DEER	3. E	3. A
4. FIRE	4. A	4. A
5. FEATHER	5. 5	5. B
6. TARGET	6. C	6. A
7. 4	7. F	7. C
8. 3	8. F	8. B
9. 5	9. T	9. C
10.5	10.F	10.A
11.2	11.T	
12.1	12.T	

IF YOU MISSED 3 QUESTIONS OR LESS CONGRATULATIONS!!!
YOU MAY NOW PRINT YOUR CERTIFICATE!!!

IF YOU MISSED 4 OR MORE QUESTIONS, GIVE ARRON ANOTHER
CHANCE BY READING THE STORY AGAIN AND REVIEW THE <u>FUN
FACTS</u>!

PLUS!

A STORY PLUS.
ENTERTAINS•EDUCATES•INSPIRES

A Story Plus
Presents

This Certificate of Achievement
To

_____

Your name

For the successful completion of the book
Arron the Royal Archer

Mister Wilson
Author Signature

ASP-14

I WON'T BE DENIED

Seems I've always known
   It didn't come suddenly
I known all along
   It was going to be

Like a burning fire
   With a wind to fan
I know this the hour
   I must take a stand

Chorus
Ooo
I won't be denied
No
I won't be denied
I must turn the tide
I won't be denied
Ooo
I won't be denied

I've given so much
   To see with my eyes
The dream I dream of
   I must realize

So step by step
   I got so far to go
To say a promise kept
   I'll give heart and soul

I've put in the time
   I've bared the pain
I'm ready to be tried
   To stake my claim

So don't push me aside
   I won't go away
I won't run and hide
   It' gone be today

By Mister Wilson

A STORY PLUS®
ENTERTAINS·EDUCATES·INSPIRES

The Perils of Cory the Caterpillar
Story: An exciting story of chances survival and transformation
Plus: Learn about the life cycle of the caterpillar and butterfly

Arron the Royal Archer
Story: A boy's triumphant adventure
Plus: Learn the origin and use of the bow and arrow

The Arrival of Grand Princess Leandria
Story: A wonderful story of the power of forgiveness
Plus: Learn about great queens

The Path of the Little Porcupine
Story: A fun story of bravery and determination
Plus: Learn about the porcupine and its defenses

The Message of the Writing Spider
Story: A rhyming story of myths to enlightenment
Plus: Learn about spiders and their webs

The Legend of Thompson the Gazelle
Story: An awesome story of leadership
Plus: Learn about the gazelle and its habitat

THE ALL NEW STANDARD OF CHILDREN BOOKS
www.astoryplus.com

ASP-16

BOOK ORDERING FORM

SCHOOL/PROGRAM _____

TEACHERS'S NAME: _____

STUDENT'S NAME: _____

ADDRESS: _____

CITY: _____ STATE: _____ ZIP CODE: _____

PHONE: _____ E-MAIL _____

BOOKS	Quantity	Price	Total
The Perils of Cory the Caterpillar			
The Message of the Writing Spider			
Arron The Royal Archer			
The Legend of Thompson the Gazelle			
The Arrival of Grand Princess Leandria			
The Path of the Little Porcupine			

Price each book $15.00

Sub Total $ _____

Sales Tax $ _____

Total $ _____

I have enclosed $ _____ (The amount totaled above) for the purchase of _____

(number of books). **Optional:** Plus an additional amount of $ _____ as a charitable contribution

toward giving a less fortunate child a book (s).

_____ Cash/Money order _____VISA _____ Master Card _____ Discover Card

Card # _____Expirations Date _____Month _____year

Parent's/Guardian _____ Date _____

THE ALL NEW STANDARD OF CHILDREN BOOKS

www.astoryplus.com

ASP-18

ASP-19

ASP-20